# SUPER CHEAT CODES AND SECRET MODES!

# READ MORE
# PRESS START!
## BOOKS!

# MORE BOOKS COMING SOON!

# PRESS START!

## SUPER CHEAT CODES AND SECRET MODES!

**THOMAS FLINTHAM**

SCHOLASTIC INC.

# FOR RICHARD AND LUCY

Copyright © 2021 by Thomas Flintham

Library of Congress Cataloging-in-Publication Data

Names: Flintham, Thomas, author, illustrator. | Flintham, Thomas. Press Start! ; 11.
Title: Super cheat codes and secret modes! / Thomas Flintham.
Description: First edition. | New York : Branches/Scholastic Inc., 2021. | Series: Press start! ; 11
Summary: A set of cheat codes unlocks a new story in the original
Super Rabbit Boy game, and Super Rabbit Boy finds himself surrounded by
King Viking's Mega Robots while his friends are in danger—and he needs
to save the day with a little help from Sunny and the secret modes.
Identifiers: LCCN 2021002901 (print)
ISBN 9781338569025 (paperback) | ISBN 9781338569032 (library binding) |
Subjects: LCSH: Superheroes—Juvenile fiction. | Supervillains—Juvenile
fiction. | Animals—Juvenile fiction. | Robots—Juvenile fiction. |
Video games—Juvenile fiction. | CYAC: Superheroes—Fiction. |
Supervillains—Fiction. | Animals—Fiction. | Robots—Fiction. |
Video games—Fiction.
Classification: LCC PZ7.1.F585 Sm 2021 (print) | LCC PZ7.1.F585 (ebook) |
DDC [Fic]—dc23
LC record available at https://lccn.loc.gov/2021002901

10 9 8 7 6 5 4 3 2 1          21 22 23 24 25

Printed in China   62
First edition, December 2021
Edited by Jess Harold
Book design by Sarah Dvojack

# TABLE OF CONTENTS

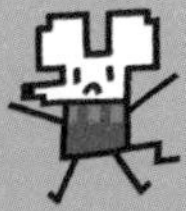

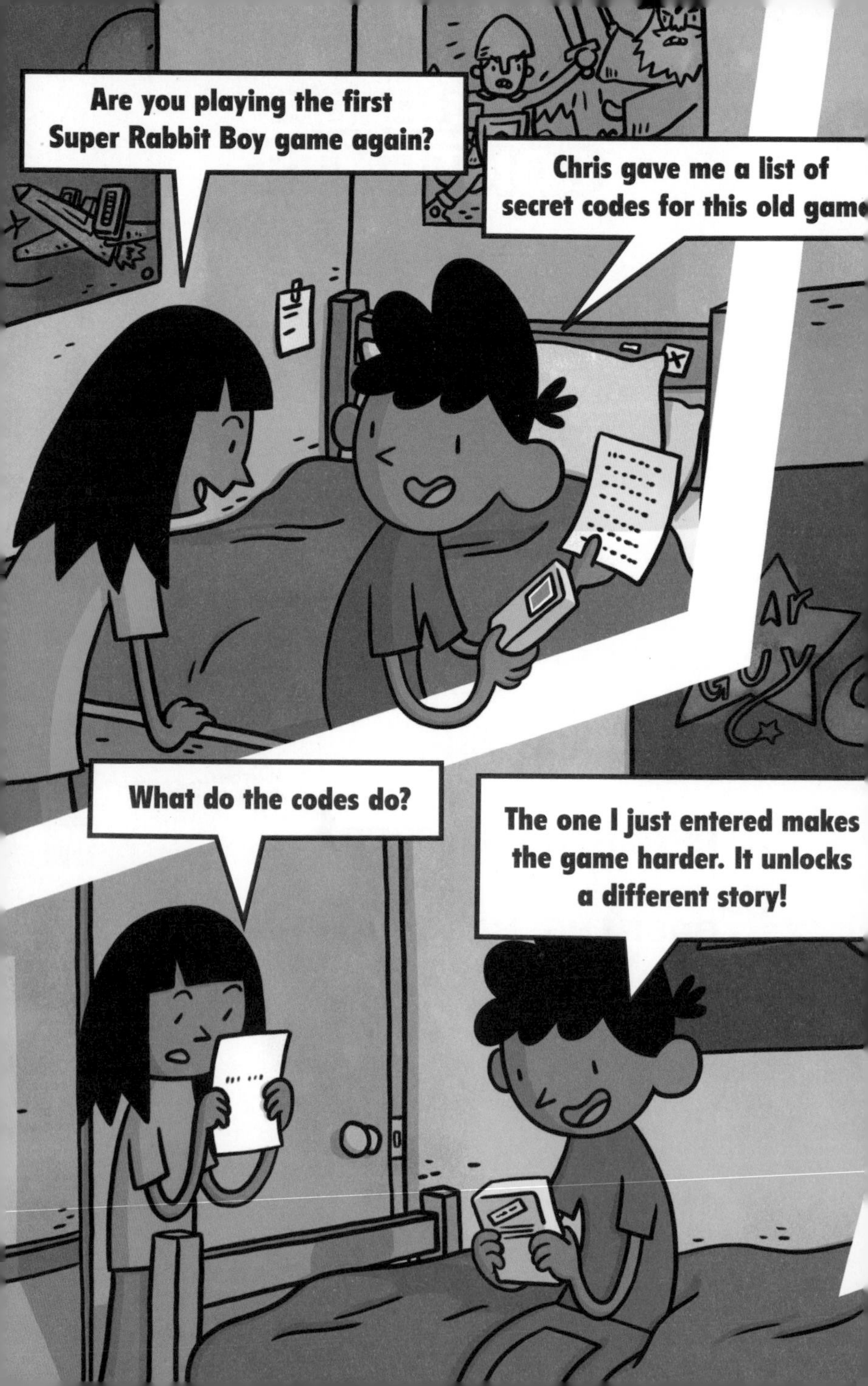

Are you playing the first Super Rabbit Boy game again?
Chris gave me a list of secret codes for this old game
What do the codes do?
The one I just entered makes the game harder. It unlocks a different story!

# 1 PRESS START!

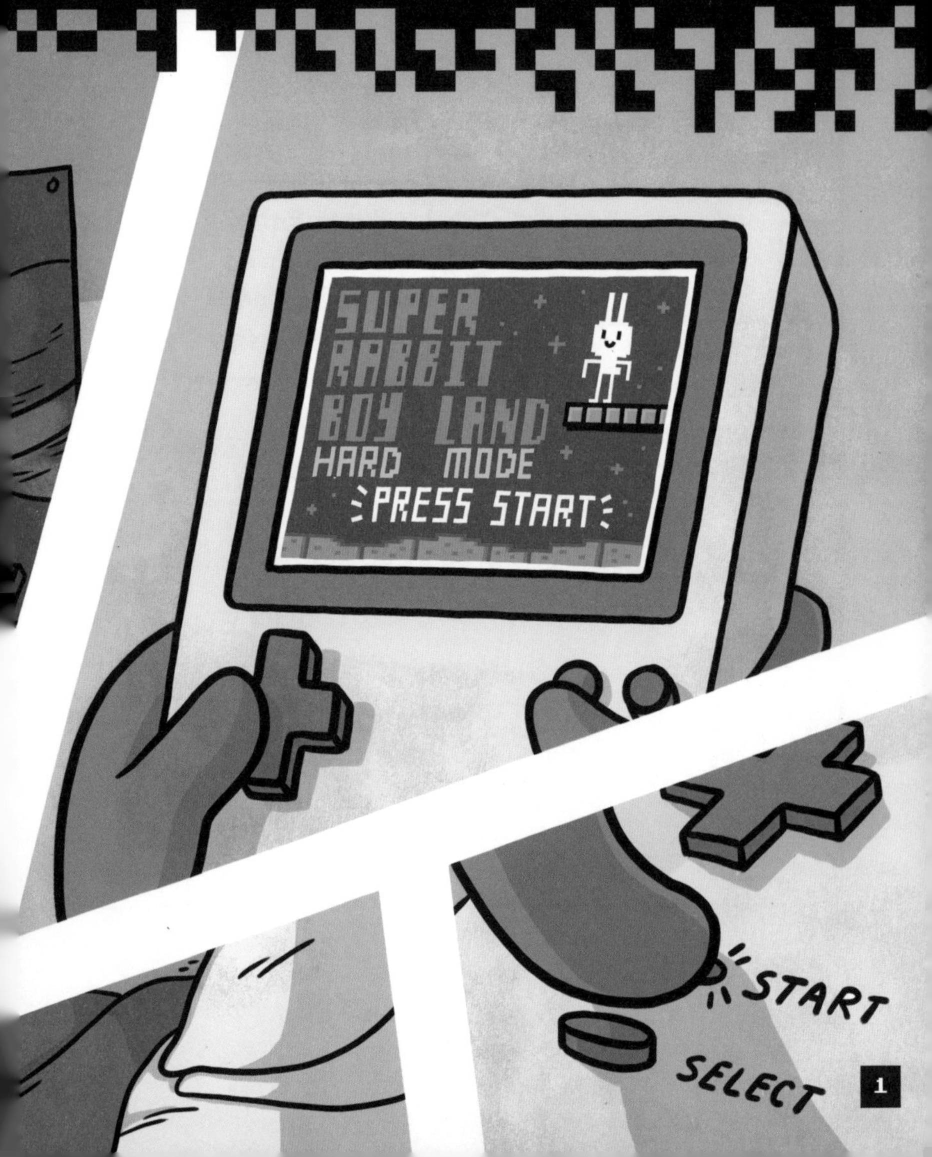
SUPER RABBIT BOY LAND
HARD MODE
PRESS START
START
SELECT

Super Rabbit Boy has just defeated King Viking and saved Singing Dog. Animal Town is having a party to celebrate.

After a long adventure, Super Rabbit Boy is happy to be back with his friends.

Meanwhile, over in Boom Boom Factory. . .
King Viking is not happy!

It's getting late in Animal Town. A large shadow appears in the sky.

King Viking is back in his hot air balloon with his Robot Army. He is ready to cause trouble in Animal Town.

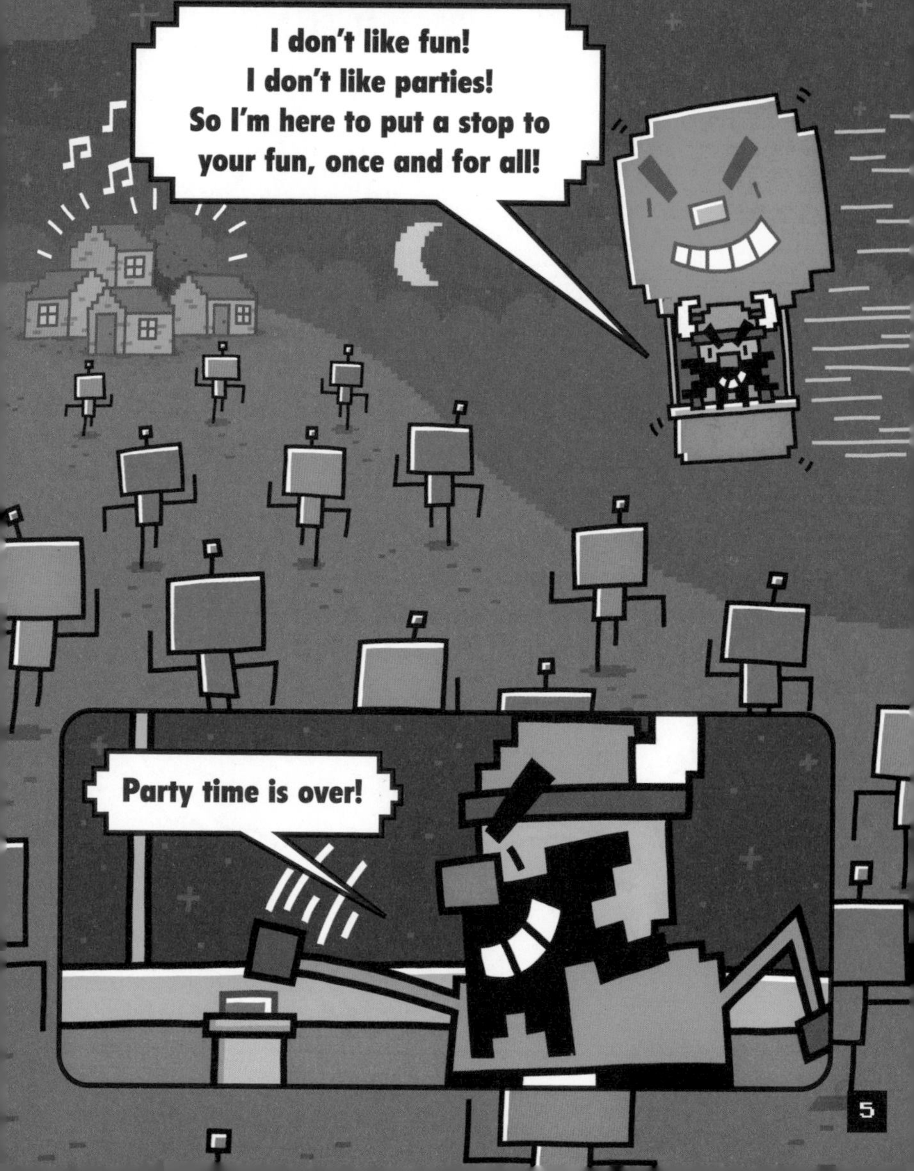
I don't like fun!
I don't like parties!
So I'm here to put a stop to your fun, once and for all!
Party time is over!

A tangle of grabbing robot arms zooms out from King Viking's hot air balloon.

Super Rabbit Boy jumps out of the way.

Eek!

He is safe. But King Viking has grabbed all his friends!

Ha! You can't have any more stinky parties if you don't have any friends to party with!

Let my friends go!

King Viking puts all of Super Rabbit Boy's friends in a giant sack. His balloon sets off toward Boom Boom Factory.

I won't let you get away with this!

Super Rabbit Boy finds himself surrounded by the new and improved robot army.

If I were you, I'd give up now! All my robots have been powered up to the max. You're no match for my Mega Robots!

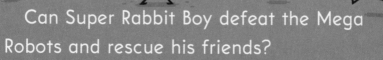

Can Super Rabbit Boy defeat the Mega Robots and rescue his friends?

# 2 BIG TROUBLE

There are six levels from Animal Town to King Viking's factory.

LEVEL 1: ANIMAL TOWN
LEVEL 2: SPLISH SPLASH SEA
LEVEL 3: SANDSTORM DESERT
LEVEL 4: CLOUDY HILLS
LEVEL 5: MOUNT BOOM
LEVEL 6: BOOM BOOM FACTORY

Before Super Rabbit Boy can set off to rescue his friends, he needs to get past the Mega Robots. He jumps into action.

Super Rabbit Boy uses his super jump to bounce on the Mega Robots.

Normally, his jump would topple King Viking's robots, but these robots are still standing.

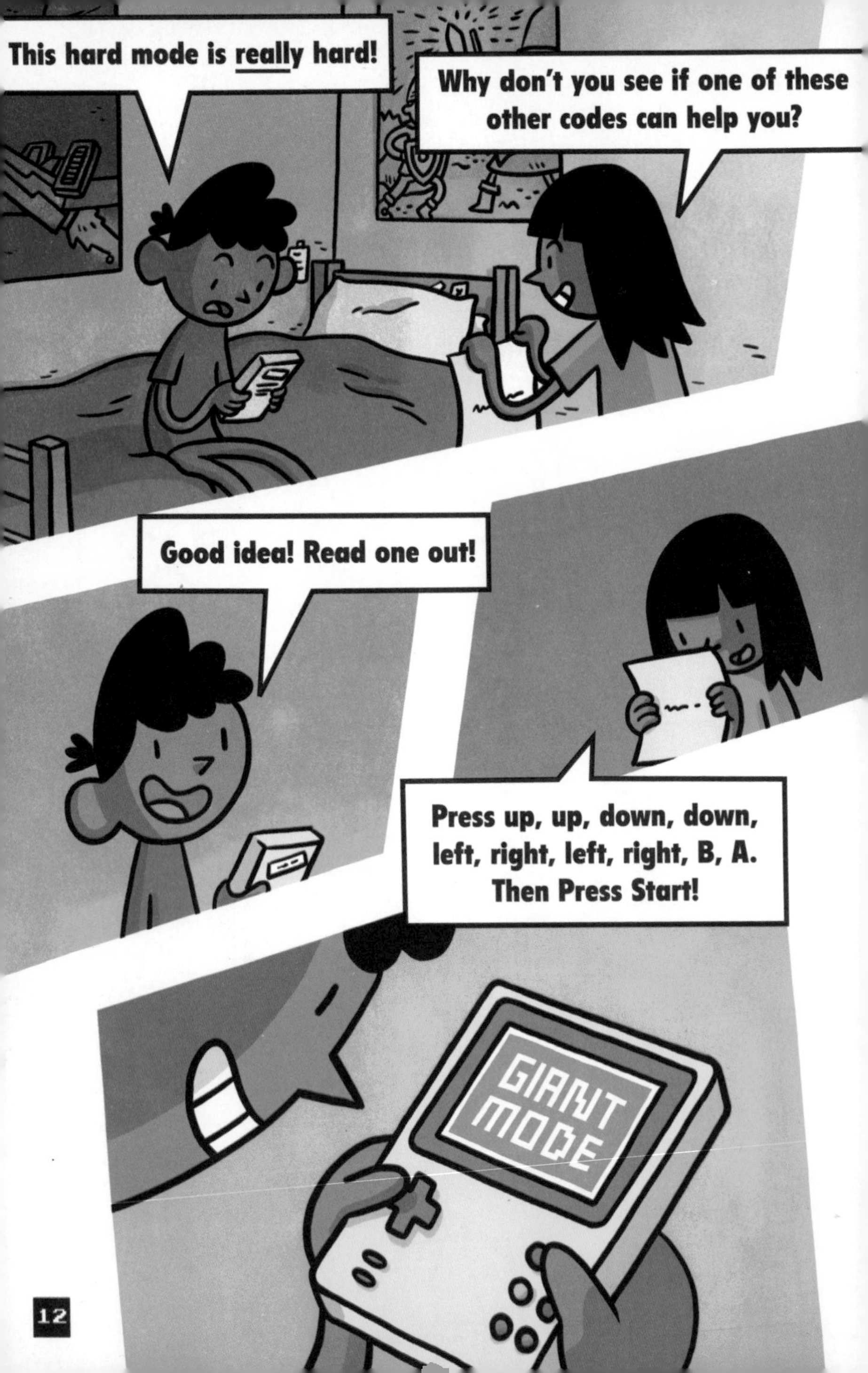
This hard mode is really hard!
Why don't you see if one of these other codes can help you?
Good idea! Read one out!
Press up, up, down, down, left, right, left, right, B, A. Then Press Start!
GIANT MODE

Suddenly, Super Rabbit Boy starts to grow and grow.

He keeps growing and growing. Getting taller and taller.

Super Rabbit Boy has turned into a GIANT!
He towers over the army of Mega Robots.

Wow! I'm a Super Sized Rabbit Boy!

The Mega Robots aren't ready to give up.
They charge toward Super Rabbit Boy.

The Mega Robots attack Super Rabbit Boy's giant feet. Their attacks don't do anything. The robots bounce right off his feet!

Now it is Super Rabbit Boy's turn to attack. He jumps high into the air.

He comes back down to the ground with a giant crash. The Mega Robots are sent flying.

They are defeated.

Super Rabbit Boy goes in search of the Exit. He takes giant strides through Animal Town.

Super Rabbit Boy finds the Exit to the next level.

But he is too big to fit through the door!

Oh no! This is a BIG problem!

Sunny, this code has "small" written next to it! Down, A, down, B, down, and then . . .

Press Start!

SMALL MODE

Suddenly, Super Rabbit Boy starts to shrink!

At first, he goes back to his normal size.

But then, he keeps getting smaller and smaller.

Super Rabbit Boy finally stops shrinking. He is tiny now!

At least I can fit through this exit door now!

Super Small Rabbit Boy steps through the door into the Splish Splash Sea level.

A giant wave crashes into Super Rabbit Boy. It throws him into the stormy sea!

# 4 IN DEEP WATER

Super Rabbit Boy is too small to swim against the tide. He gets washed through the level. Robo-Fish snap at Super Rabbit Boy as he gets pulled past them.

Eek!

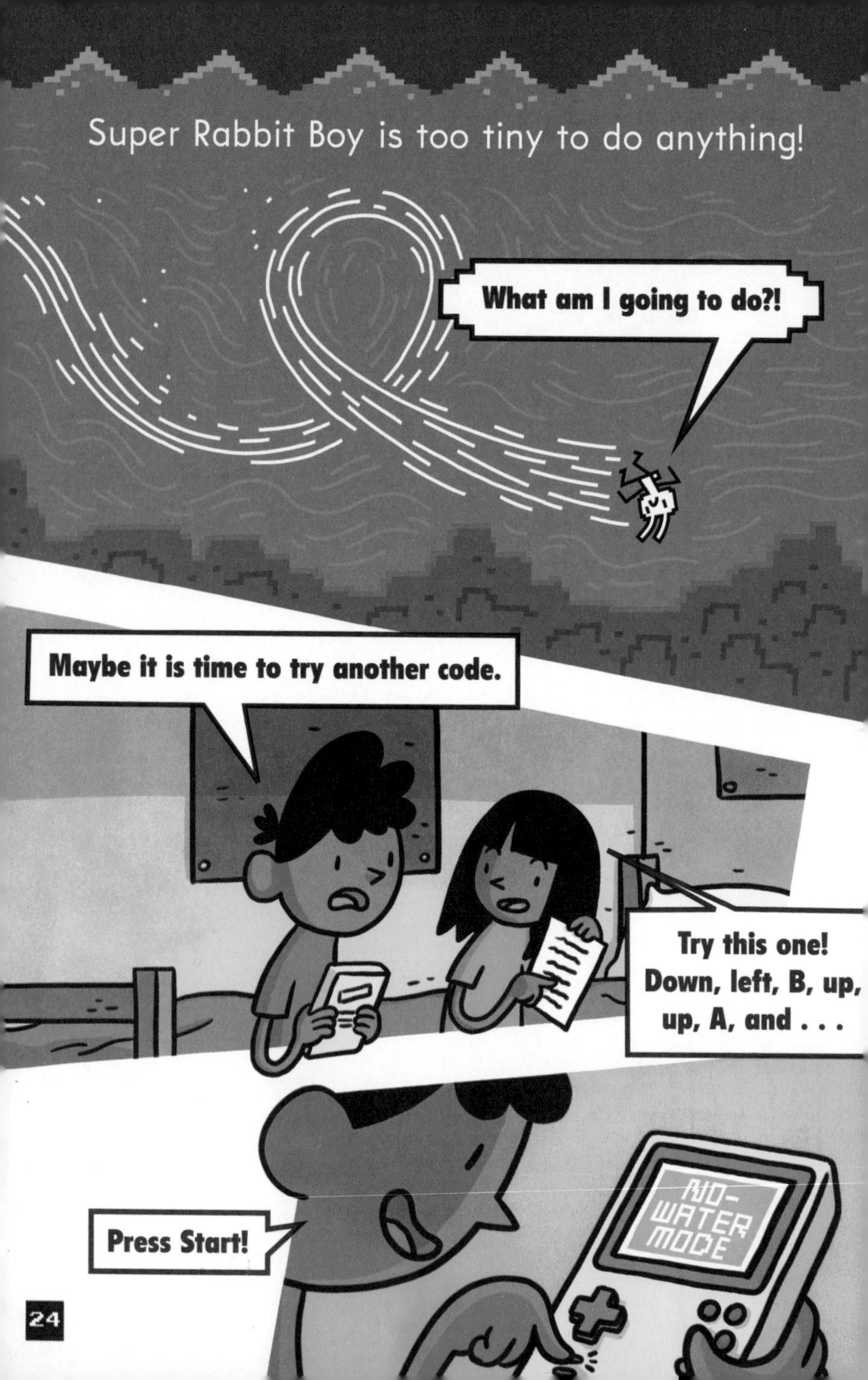
Super Rabbit Boy is too tiny to do anything!
What am I going to do?!
Maybe it is time to try another code.
Try this one! Down, left, B, up, up, A, and . . .
Press Start!
NO-WATER MODE

Super Rabbit Boy is suddenly sitting on the sea floor. All the water has disappeared!

He carefully hops over the Robo-Fish. He is still very small, but the fish can't move without the water.

Super Rabbit Boy spots the Exit. It is on a platform high above him.

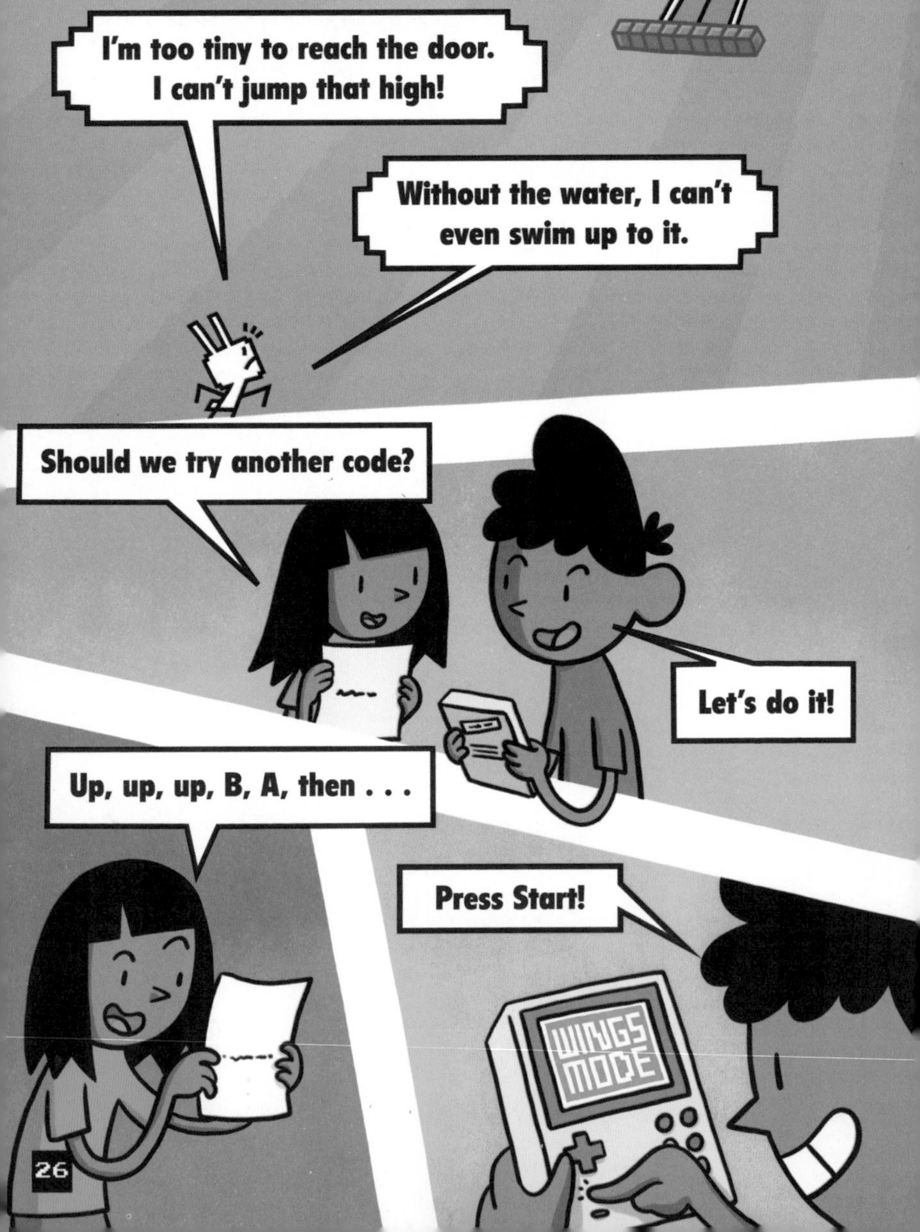
I'm too tiny to reach the door. I can't jump that high!
Without the water, I can't even swim up to it.
Should we try another code?
Let's do it!
Up, up, up, B, A, then . . .
Press Start!
WINGS MODE

In a flash of light, Super Rabbit Boy is back to his normal size, and he has grown wings!

Using his new wings, Super Flying Rabbit Boy flies up to the Exit.

# FLYING HIGH!

Super Rabbit Boy flies into Level 3,
Sandstorm Desert.

I thought the desert would be hot,
but it's very cold here! I had better
get out quickly before I freeze!

Super Rabbit Boy is flying high in the sky.

There are Robo-Lizards on the ground, but they can't reach him.

Super Rabbit Boy quickly finds the Exit.

He swoops down toward the door. The ground beneath him starts to shake.

A giant Mega Robo-Snake leaps out of the ground into the air!

It almost catches Super Rabbit Boy in its jaws.

Super Rabbit Boy swoops toward the Exit again. The Mega Robo-Snake is right behind him.

Super Rabbit Boy makes it through the door just in time.

I'm lucky I had these wings. I'm not sure how I would have gotten away without them!

Super Rabbit Boy has entered the next level, Cloudy Hills. It is very windy!

Super Rabbit Boy can see Mount Boom in the distance.

Super Rabbit Boy hops in the air, ready to fly to the mountaintop!

As soon as he starts to fly, he gets caught in the strong winds. He is thrown back down to the ground.

Ow! This level might be harder than I thought!

It's too windy here! These wings won't work. I need another code!

Try this one! Press left, right, left, right, left, left, right, right, A, then . . .

Press Start!

STRETCH MODE

Super Rabbit Boy's wings disappear. His arms and legs go wobbly.

He moves his arms. They stretch out until they are <u>really</u> long!

He moves his legs. They stretch out, too!

Ha! This feels really weird!

I have an idea!

Super Stretchy Rabbit Boy uses his stretchy arms and legs to reach the next platform. He steps across.

Super Rabbit Boy uses his long limbs to make his way through the level. He stretches from platform to platform.

The wind howls around him, but he makes sure he's always holding on to something.

Finally, he finds the Exit. He grabs the doorframe and pulls himself through.

# BASHING BOSS BONANZA

Super Rabbit Boy is on top of Mount Boom. He can see Boom Boom Factory high above him.

It's time to get inside King Viking's factory!

Super Rabbit Boy uses his stretchy legs to step across the lake of lava.

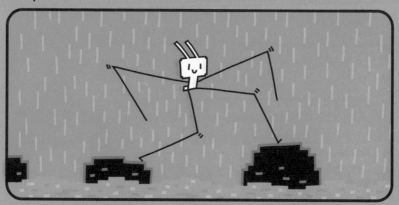

Fireballs and robots leap toward him. Super Rabbit Boy can barely dodge them.

It is hard to move fast with these long arms and legs!

Super Rabbit Boy is almost at Boom Boom Factory. But he sees two giant Robots ready to stop him.

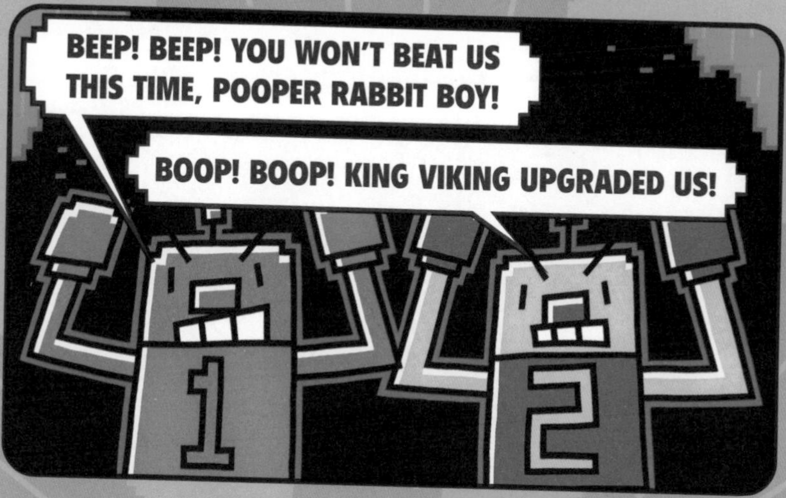
BEEP! BEEP! YOU WON'T BEAT US THIS TIME, POOPER RABBIT BOY!
BOOP! BOOP! KING VIKING UPGRADED US!

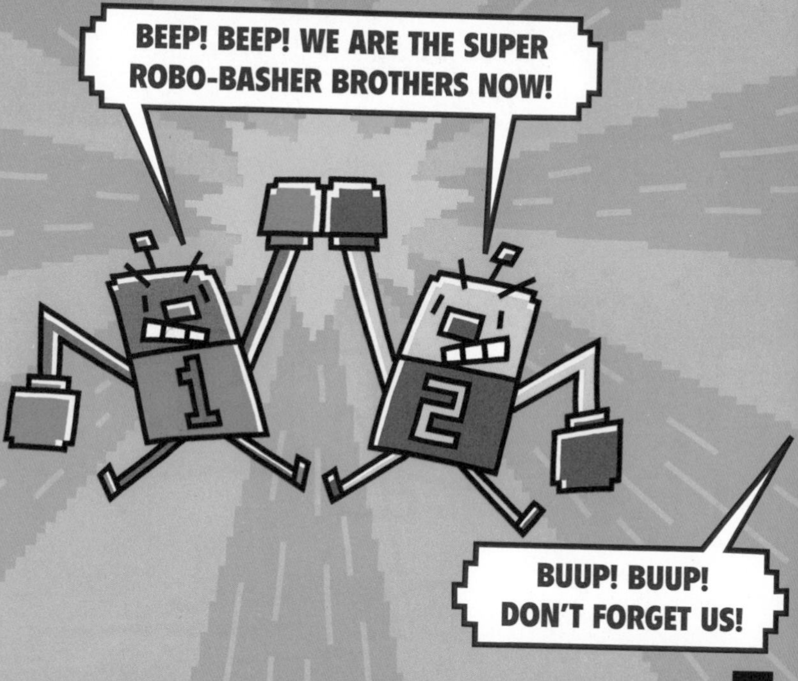
BEEP! BEEP! WE ARE THE SUPER ROBO-BASHER BROTHERS NOW!
BUUP! BUUP! DON'T FORGET US!

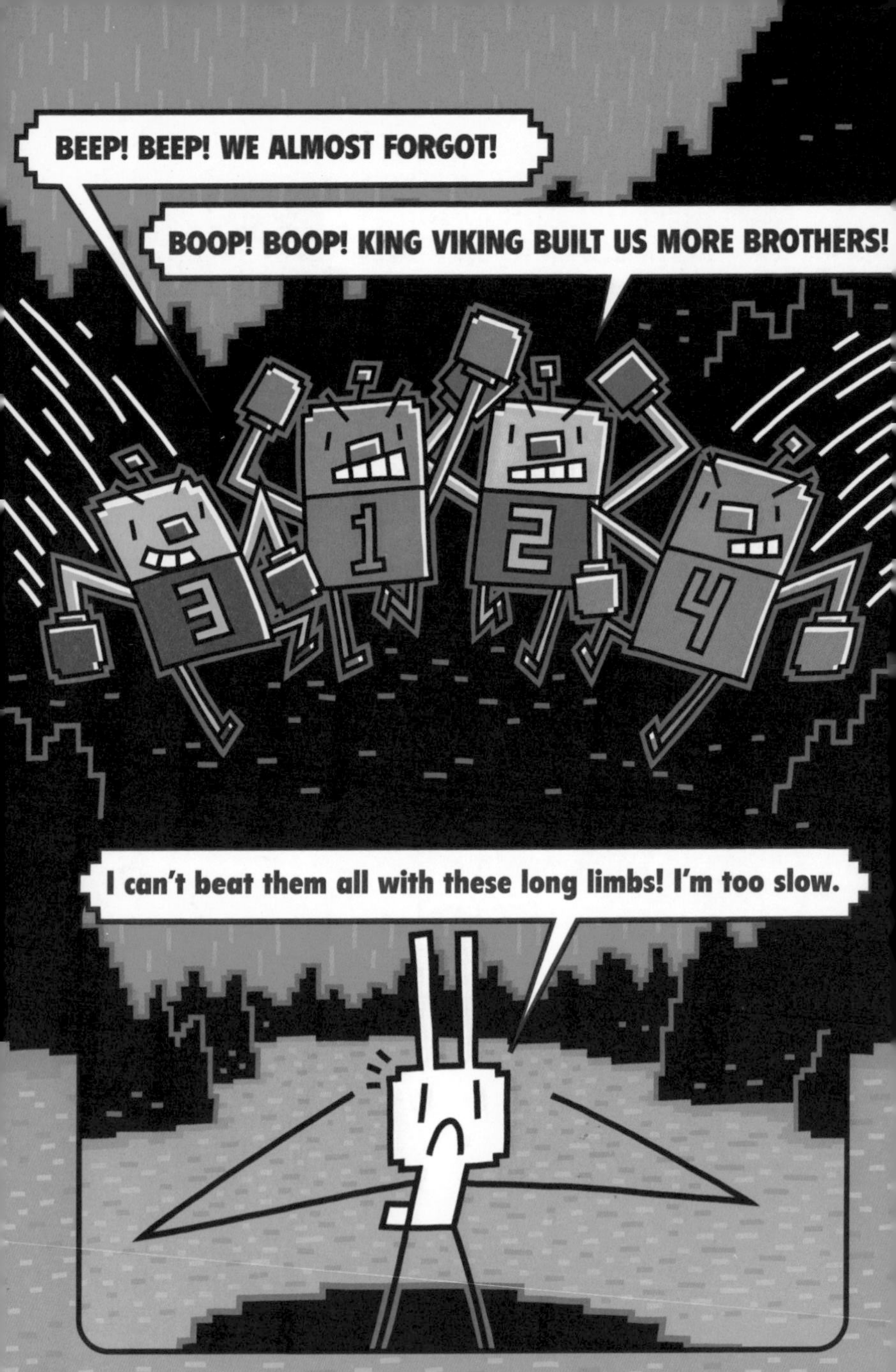
BEEP! BEEP! WE ALMOST FORGOT!
BOOP! BOOP! KING VIKING BUILT US MORE BROTHERS!
I can't beat them all with these long limbs! I'm too slow.

# 8 TEAM SPIRIT

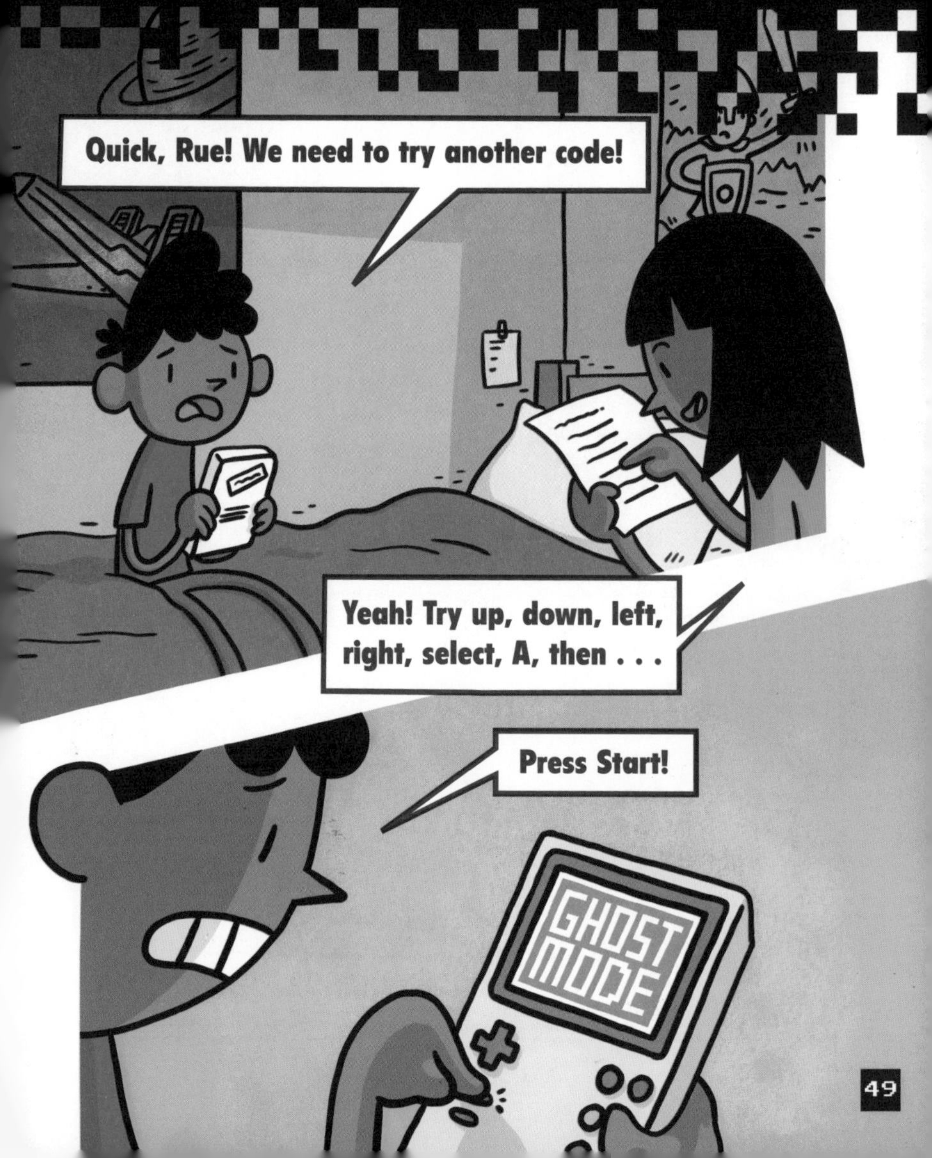
Quick, Rue! We need to try another code!
Yeah! Try up, down, left, right, select, A, then . . .
Press Start!
GHOST MODE

Super Rabbit Boy turns into a ghost!

The Super Robo-Basher Brothers all dive at Super Ghost Rabbit Boy. But they go flying through his ghost body.

The Robots charge forward again.

BIIP! BIIP! QUICK, BROTHERS! TRY AGAIN!

Super Ghost Rabbit Boy has an idea. He floats toward the edge of the lake.

Maybe being a ghost isn't a bad thing!

The Robots fly through Super Rabbit Boy again. This time, they fall straight into the lake of lava!

With the Super Robo-Basher Brothers defeated, Super Rabbit Boy floats toward Boom Boom Factory.

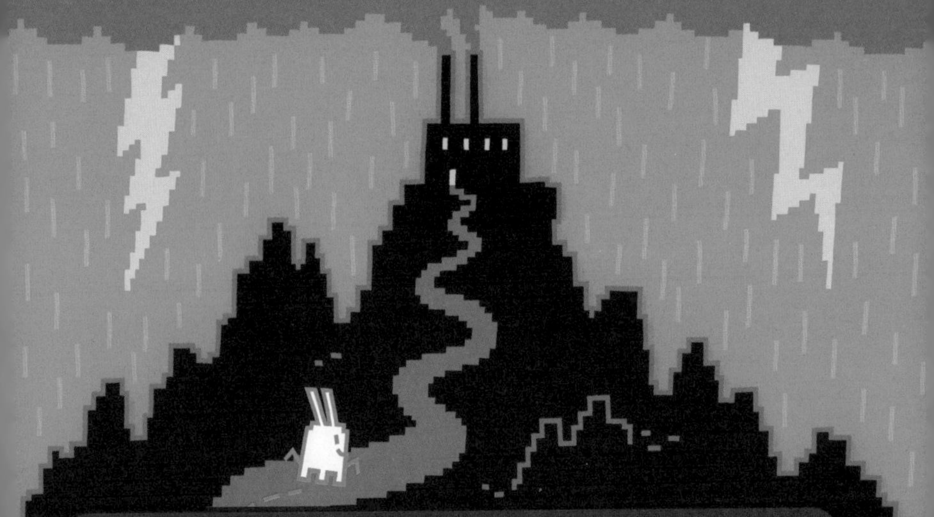

As a ghost, he can't touch the door. So he floats through it instead!

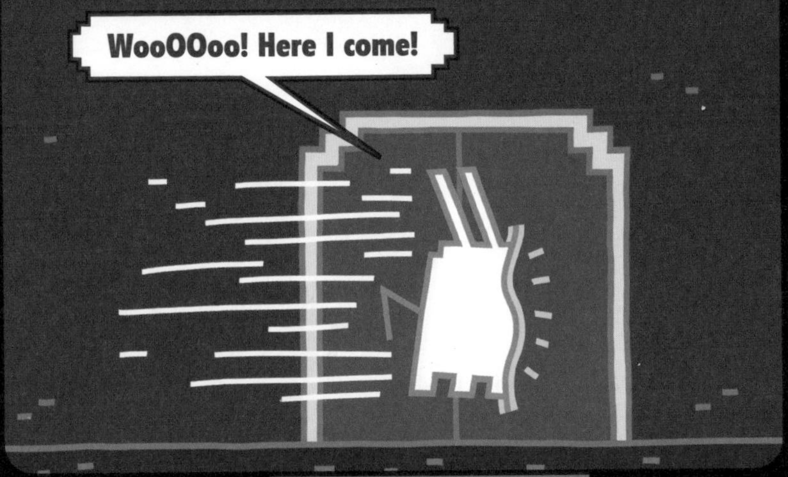
WooOOoo! Here I come!

# 9 HAUNTING THE HALLS

Super Rabbit Boy is inside Boom Boom Factory at last.

Time to save my friends!

Boom Boom Factory is like a maze. King Viking has filled it with Mega Robots. Super Rabbit Boy uses his ghost powers to float past them.

Ha! I could get used to being a ghost!

Super Rabbit Boy reaches a dead end.

Then he has an idea. Because he is a ghost, he can just float through the walls!

Without any walls blocking his way, Super Rabbit Boy quickly finds the door to King Viking's Super Secret Office.

Super Rabbit Boy floats inside. The room is very dark.

King Viking! Where are you? And where are my friends?

I'm right here and . . .

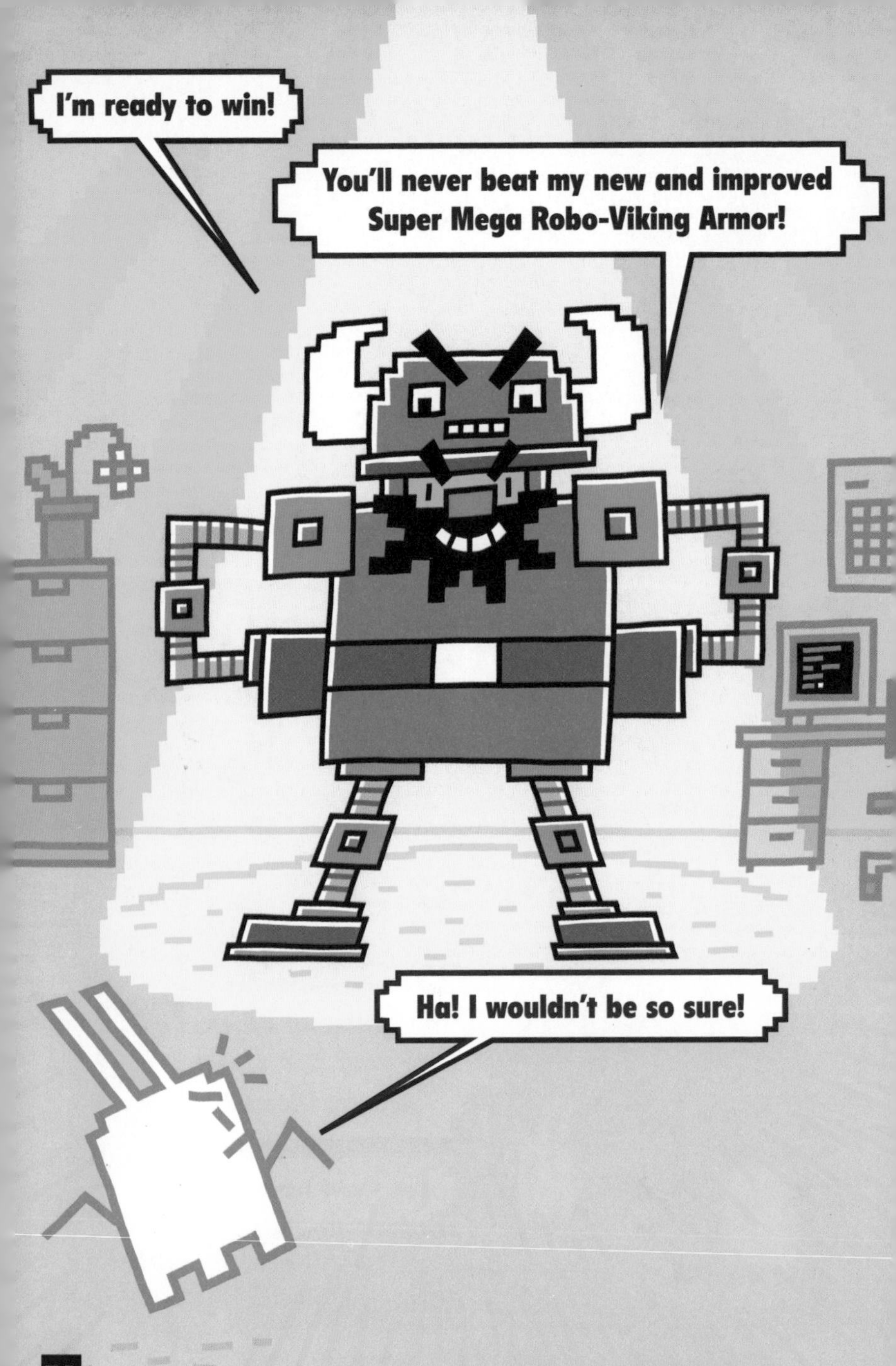
I'm ready to win!
You'll never beat my new and improved Super Mega Robo-Viking Armor!
Ha! I wouldn't be so sure!

Super Rabbit Boy floats into action. But his ghostly attacks go right through the Super Mega Robo-Viking Armor.

Oh no! I can't strike a blow!

I don't think I can win if I'm a ghost!

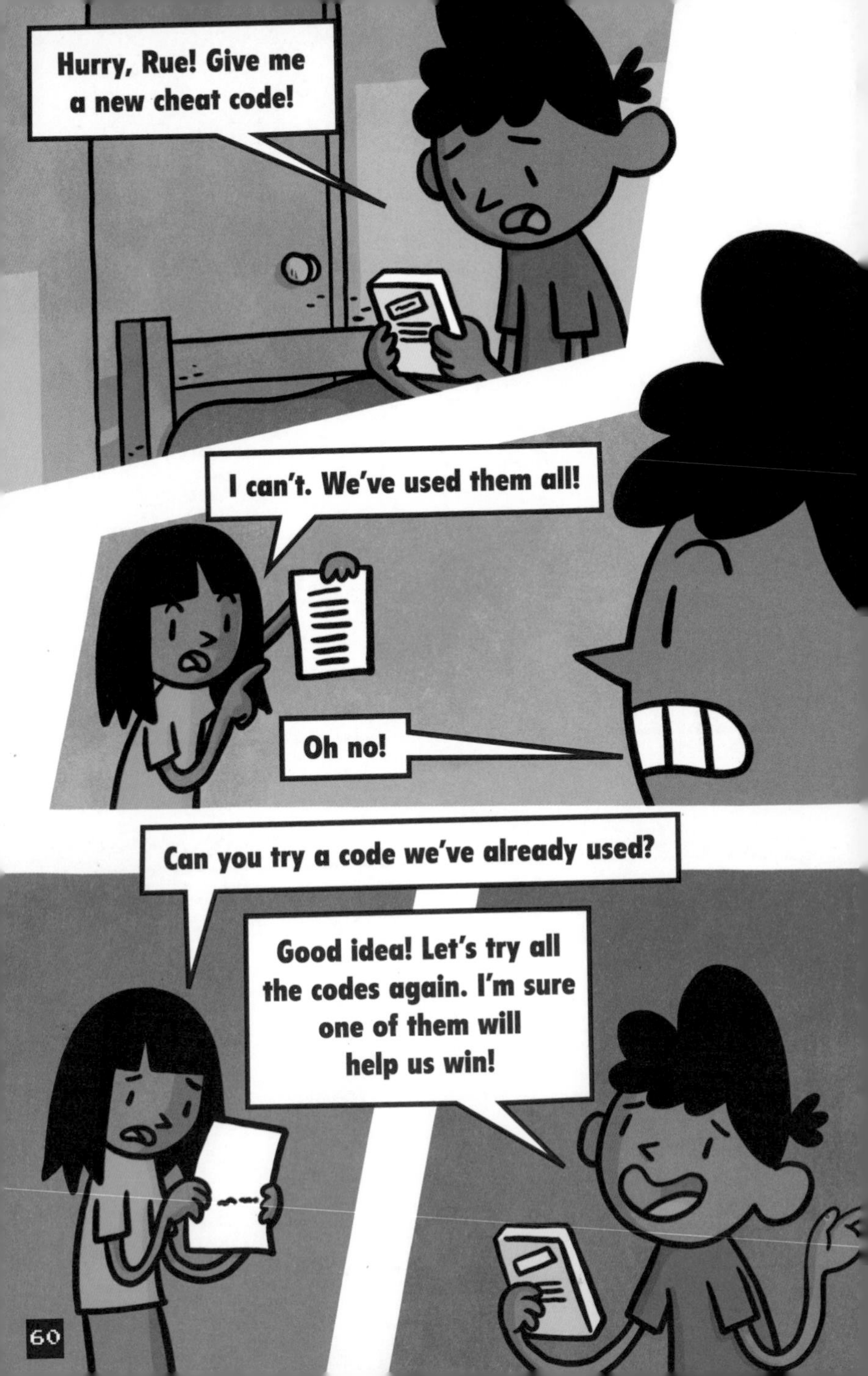
Hurry, Rue! Give me a new cheat code!
I can't. We've used them all!
Oh no!
Can you try a code we've already used?
Good idea! Let's try all the codes again. I'm sure one of them will help us win!

Super Rabbit Boy isn't a ghost anymore.
He starts growing again!

Oh no! I don't think this will work!

Super Rabbit Boy is giant sized again, but
King Viking's Super Secret Office has a low
ceiling. He doesn't fit in the room!

In a flash, Super Rabbit Boy is tiny again! He's far too small to fight King Viking now!

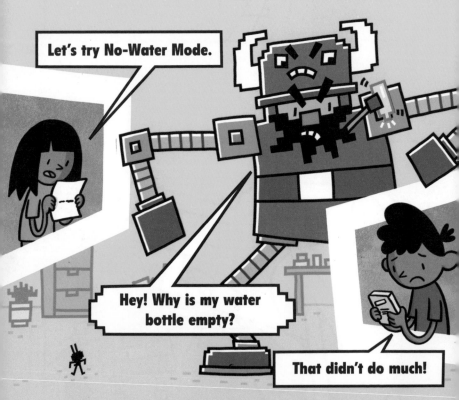

Let's try No-Water Mode.

Hey! Why is my water bottle empty?

That didn't do much!

Can Super Rabbit Boy find a way to win?

# 10 THE FINAL MODE

Super Rabbit Boy has wings again. He flies toward King Viking, ready to attack.

This is more like it!

The Super Mega Robo-Viking Armor is too quick for Super Rabbit Boy. It swings its powerful arms through the air. Super Rabbit Boy dodges just in time.

In a flash, Super Rabbit Boy is stretchy
again. He reaches up and grabs King Viking.

King Viking easily throws him off.

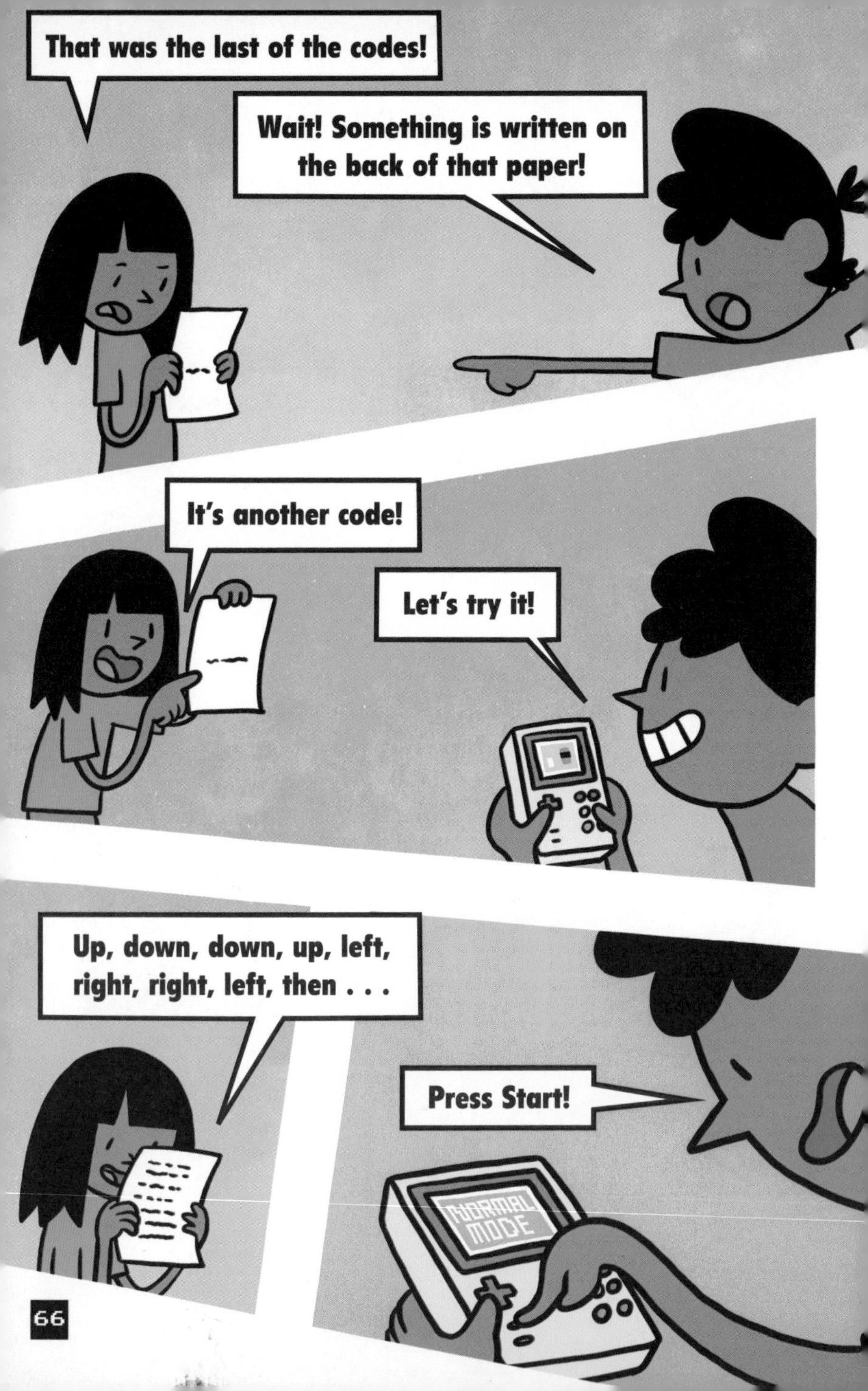

That was the last of the codes!
Wait! Something is written on the back of that paper!
It's another code!
Let's try it!
Up, down, down, up, left, right, right, left, then . . .
Press Start!
NORMAL MODE

Super Rabbit Boy is back to normal. He isn't big or small. He can't fly or stretch. He isn't a ghost.

Super Rabbit Boy uses his super jump to leap back into action.

King Viking swings the Super Mega Robo-Viking Armor's fist. Super Rabbit Boy leaps over it.

Super Rabbit Boy has an idea. He hops up on top of the Super Mega Robo-Viking Armor!

King Viking swings both fists at Super Rabbit Boy!

Super Rabbit Boy jumps out of the way just in time. The Super Mega Robo-Viking Armor punches itself and explodes! King Viking is sent flying out through the ceiling!

Super Rabbit Boy frees all his friends.
He has saved the day again!

Back in Animal Town, Super Rabbit Boy's
friends throw a party to celebrate.

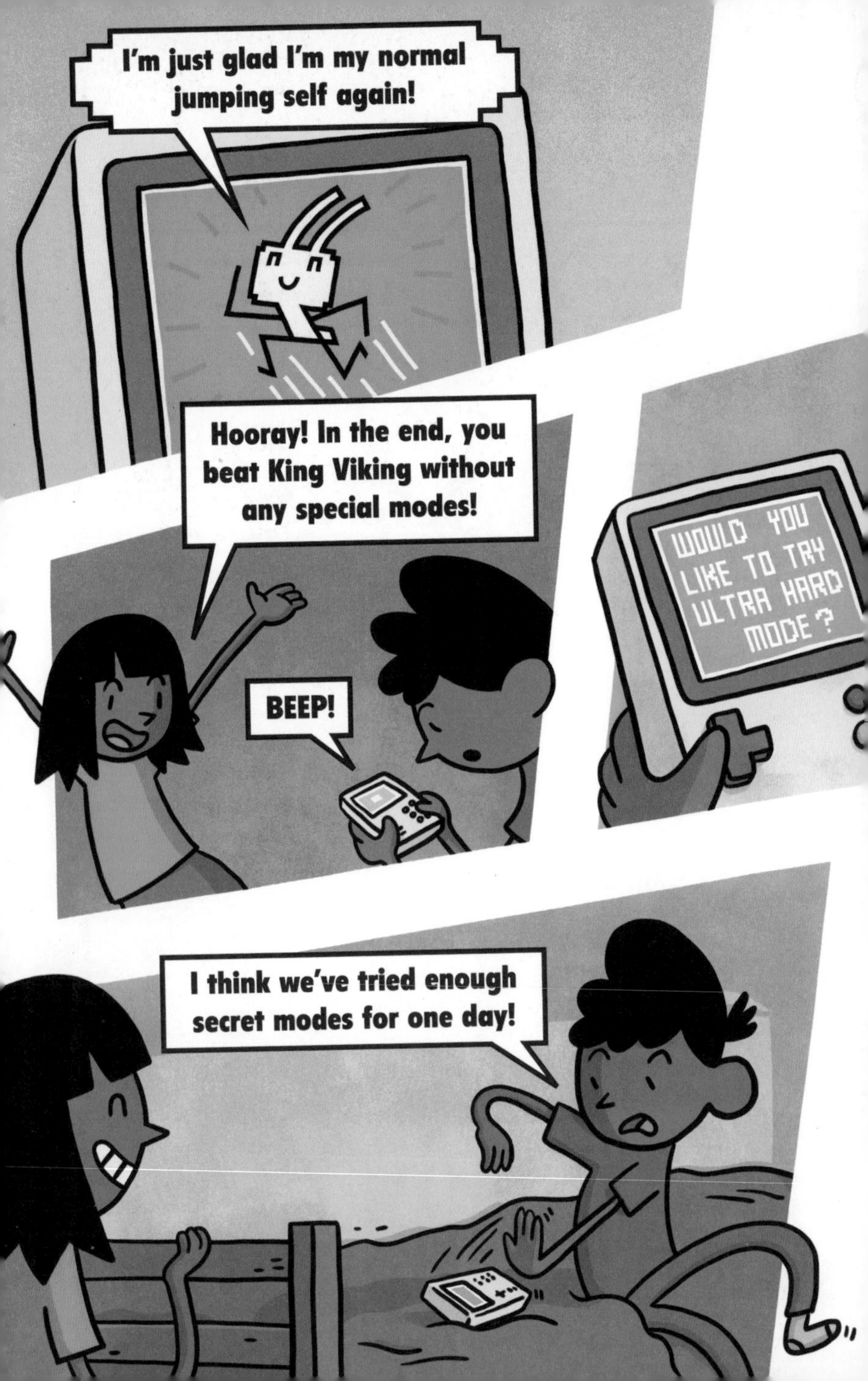
I'm just glad I'm my normal jumping self again!
Hooray! In the end, you beat King Viking without any special modes!
BEEP!
WOULD YOU LIKE TO TRY ULTRA HARD MODE?
I think we've tried enough secret modes for one day!

# THOMAS FLINTHAM

has always loved to draw and tell stories, and now that is his job! He grew up in Lincoln, England, and studied illustration in Camberwell, London. He lives by the sea with his dog, Ziggy, in Cornwall.

Thomas is the creator of THOMAS FLINTHAM'S BOOK OF MAZES AND PUZZLES and many other books for kids. PRESS START! is his first early chapter book series.

**The secret codes have changed Super Rabbit Boy's world in many ways. How many differences can you find? What things stay the same?**

# PRESS START!

How much do you know about

## SUPER CHEAT CODES AND SECRET MODES!?

King Viking doesn't like fun or parties. How does he put a stop to the celebration in Animal Town?

Super Rabbit Boy uses Small Mode to leave the Animal Town level. Does this mode help when he gets to the Splish Splash Sea level? Why or why not?

Super Rabbit Boy thinks the Sandstorm Desert level is easy to travel through. Why does he think this? Does his opinion change?

Why is Ghost Mode so helpful on the Boom Boom Factory level?

In the final battle, Sunny uses all the different modes to help Super Rabbit Boy beat King Viking. What happens when he tries to use No-Water Mode? (Hint: check page 62!)

31901067302473